God
Bless,
Tara
& Peter

Peter the Shih-Poo

Sometimes Everyone Needs a Little Help From Above!

Tara Chaudry Kovalski

Peter the Shih-Poo
by Tara Chaudry Kovalski
Copyright ©2017 Tara Chaudry Kovalski

ISBN 978-1-58169-660-8
For Worldwide Distribution
Printed in the U.S.A.

Based on a true story.
Illustrated by Joe McCormick

Gazelle Press
P.O. Box 191540 • Mobile, AL 36619
800-367-8203

Dedication

To my precious daughter, Lily Grace, my sweet nephew Dylan,
and every little girl and boy in God's Kingdom.
"All your children shall be taught by the Lord, and great shall be
the peace of your children." Isaiah 54:13

Acknowledgments

To the Lord—my spiritual Father, trusted advisor, leader, healer, Savior, and friend. I offer my first book as Your first fruit and place it on Your altar. Your will be done. Thank You for giving me purpose.

To my beloved husband, Brian—my spiritual partner, supporter, protector, encourager, and best friend. Thank you for enabling me to follow my passion.

To my dog, Peter—my creative inspiration, messenger, and gift from God. Thank you for being an endless source of joy and comfort.

To my late father, Jamshed Chaudry—my longstanding supporter, motivator, protector, and provider. I will always admire your Christ-like selflessness. You did without so that I could be blessed in ways you could only imagine.

To my pastor, Jon Winter—my spiritual mother, teacher, confidante, and healer. Christ brought you into my life to hold my hand, and you never let go. Thank you for showing me how to put on my spiritual armor, take up my cross, and walk in victory.

To my spiritual advisor, Mary Johnson—my teacher, encourager, healer, and friend. I will never forget the time you received discernment from the Lord about my call to write and publish. Thank you for helping me navigate many spiritual obstacles so that I can now share the Good News.

To my agent, Keith Carroll, Gazelle Press, and Illustrator, Joe McCormick—thank you for having faith in my message so that together we can spread the Good News.

Sometimes when God wants to remind us of His love, He sends us a dog. This dog acts as His messenger and lives on Earth to teach us, protect us, and love us. Peter the Shih-Poo lived in Heaven.

God had a special plan for Peter to
help a little girl on Earth, but...
was Peter ready to move?
And, was the little girl
ready for Peter?

"Rise and shine, Peter!" said
Top Dog. "God wants to speak with you
in Bark Botanical Garden."

"Aw, do I have to?" Peter sighed. "I'm
hungry. Please send up a rawhide."

"For breakfast?! Rawhides are for snacks. I'll
have breakfast ready when you return.
Now, run along. You don't want to keep
God waiting."

"Come closer, Peter," said a gentle but commanding voice from beyond the lush garden. "Do you know why I sent for you?"

"Not really," Peter said as he rubbed his eyes. "I was actually in the middle of a really good dream where I ate rawhides for breakfast, lunch, and dinner."

"Sorry to disturb you, but I'd like to present you with a very important assignment. How would you like to live on Earth and become a companion to a little girl?"

"Can I still eat rawhides and play all day?" asked Peter.

"Maybe," said God. "But there will be some work for you to do. You will have responsibilities."

"But I already have responsibilities in Heaven," Peter replied. "My job is to eat rawhides and play all day."

"Very funny!" God laughed. "Now, look at the big screen and watch what is happening in little Taylor's life."

Back on Earth, the leaves were starting to fall from the trees. A little girl sat on the cold floor of an animal hospital, crying next to a cage. Telly, her ten-year-old black cat, was very sick. The vet could not heal him. Taylor felt alone and helpless as she cradled him.

"What's wrong with him?" Peter asked God, concerned.

"He's dying. Telly has been Taylor's companion for a long time, but now I want him to live in Heaven."

"But why?"

"I have my reasons," said God, "and they are not always meant for you to know. Life on Earth isn't like it is in Heaven, where you can stay the same age and play all day. On Earth, everyone grows up and changes. Everyone has a special purpose. When it is complete, I call them home to live with Me."

When Peter looked again, he saw Taylor leaving the animal hospital with her brother. Telly was wrapped in a blanket. Taylor's brother drove them home and dug a big hole in the backyard. Taylor hugged Telly, placed him in a little box, and put it into the hole. They filled the hole with dirt and decorated the gravesite with yellow marigolds and plastic butterflies. Yellow was the color of Telly's eyes.

"So, Telly will live in Heaven now?" Peter asked.

"That is correct," said God.

"Taylor will get another cat, right? She doesn't need me. Well, I'm late for play group with the other small dogs. Gotta run."

"Not so fast, Peter. Keep watching the big screen."

Now there was snow on the ground. The holidays were fast approaching, but Taylor was quiet and withdrawn. She didn't want to spend time with her family or play with her toys.

One day, Taylor's brother took her out for an afternoon drive. They went to the pet store to buy fish for his aquarium. Taylor moped behind her brother as they walked into the store. She went because her parents told her to go, but she would rather have stayed home.

They went to the aquatic section and looked at the brightly colored fish. Taylor thought they were pretty, especially the bright yellow ones. But yellow reminded her of Telly's eyes, and she began to feel sad. Just as they headed for the checkout line, a puppy with dark brown hair came out of nowhere, stood on its hind legs, and greeted Taylor with a big smile and a little yip. Taylor grinned. She was happy to see such a cute dog and thought to herself, "If I ever get a dog someday, I want one just like this."

"What kind of dog is this?" she asked the store lady.

"Oh, he's a Shih Tzu Poodle. A Shih-Poo for short. Would you like to pet him?"

"For sure," Taylor said excitedly.

When Taylor got home, she thought about the cute little dog she met in the pet store. She really enjoyed meeting him. That night before bed, she knelt down and began to say her prayers:

"Hi, God. It was so nice to meet the little doggy today, but I still miss Telly. I don't want to miss him so much. Please heal my broken heart. Thanks. Amen."

Before she fell asleep, lying in her bed, Taylor heard a faint whisper from within. It said softly, "Let him go." At first, she wasn't sure what it meant. After she thought about it, she wondered if the gentle voice was God's way of getting her attention—that it was time to stop thinking about Telly so much. Maybe she was still holding on too tightly. Maybe it was time to release Telly from her heart.

After she fell asleep, Taylor had a vivid dream. She saw Telly eating tuna fish, his favorite treat, and playing mousey, his favorite game, in Bark Botanical Garden. He was happy and doing backflips.

When she woke the next morning, a ray
of sunlight beamed through the window and shone on
her face. Today would be a new day. She could feel it.
Today she would have fun playing.

A couple months later, the spring flowers started to
bloom.

Taylor still thought about Telly from time to time,
but her heart didn't feel as heavy. She knew
that Telly would want her to be happy and play.
And, she knew that Telly was okay.

"Yay!" Peter exclaimed. "She's all better!"

"But she will face more tough times in the future," God told him, "and she will need a friend whom she can trust.

"She will need someone to comfort her during times of need and to remind her of My love."

"Oh," Peter sighed. "I don't want her to feel alone. She seems like a pretty neat girl. I'm in. Can I get a first class seat on the ride down to Earth?"

"Sure," God replied.

Back on Earth, it was a week before Easter.
Taylor and her older brother decided to go shopping at a new neighborhood mall. Taylor loved looking in store windows.
On the way to the ice cream shop, they passed by a pet store that had little cribs in the window. Each crib contained a cute little puppy.

Taylor went inside to look around, just for fun. She immediately spotted a fluffy, white and tan Shih Tzu Poodle playing with a chew toy in the first crib. When their eyes met, Taylor felt warm and tingly all over. She asked the store owner if she could hold him.

As soon as the puppy was placed in her arms, her heart lept for joy. Taylor knew he was meant for her. She even heard the gentle voice inside her say, "His name will be Peter."

When she got permission from her parents, they brought Peter home. Taylor couldn't wait to introduce Peter to his new home. When they pulled up to the house, Peter jumped out of the car and ran to the front door.

As soon as they were inside, Peter ran upstairs to Taylor's bedroom and sat outside the door.

"How did he know where to go?" Taylor wondered. "You are so special. You're exactly what I wanted."

As Peter gazed into her eyes,
Taylor felt pretty special too.

"I feel so happy with you, Peter."

Peter climbed into her lap and
began licking her cheek.

"God answered my prayers
when He gave you to me."

Peter wagged his tail
in agreement.

"Oh, what fun we will have together. I can't wait to teach you new tricks, but something tells me that you will teach me a thing or two."

That night, Taylor said her prayers and thanked God for bringing Peter into her life. Peter had a rawhide treat before bed.

"Sweet dreams, my sweet puppy."

"This is Heaven," Peter thought to himself as he dozed off to sleep.

And that is the story
of how God gave a little girl the gift of
a special dog. This little dog would be with
her through the good times and
the bad, to remind her that God
cares for her and that His
love is always with her.

About the Author

Tara Chaudry Kovalski is an attorney from Crownsville, MD, where she resides with her husband, Brian, their daughter, Lily Grace, and a Shih Tzu Poodle named Peter. Peter came into Tara's life at a time when she needed to feel God's love and comfort the most. Since that divine meeting in the spring of 2011, her life has changed for the better. Peter helps enable Tara to pursue her creative passions for writing, photography, and community service.

Tara and Peter enjoy raising money for animal charities in the Maryland, Washington DC, and Virginia areas. Peter is also a registered pet-facilitated therapy dog. He brings a smile to just about everyone he meets!

Peter the Shih-Poo is Tara's first children's book. For more information about Peter, visit his website: www.petertheshihpoo.com. Feel free to like his Facebook Fan Page, Peter the Shih-Poo, and follow his adventures on Instagram @petertheshihpoo, where you will find a plethora of adorably witty photos taken by Tara.

To contact the author:
tchaud4@hotmail.com

Artwork by Joe McCormick
http://www.joemccormickcountry.com